About the Author

Francesca Theodorou has always been a bit of an introvert. The only way she could express herself or have some kind of release, was from writing her poetry. The more she started to write, the more poetry flowed, making it easier for her to express herself in and out of her poems, making it a part of who she is today.

This book is dedicated to you. The you who is afraid to be true to yourself. The you who is afraid to be real to yourself and others. Let it go and let it be.

Francesca Theodorou

Behind the Mask

A CIP catalogue record for this title is available from the British Library.

ISBN 9781786127495 (Paperback)
ISBN 9781786127501 (Hardback)
ISBN 9781786127518 (E-Book)

www.austinmacauley.com

First Published (2016)
Austin Macauley Publishers Ltd.
25 Canada Square
Canary Wharf
London
E14 5LQ

Survival of the Fittest

I saw something I should not have seen
That most of you would have regretted
But for some strange reason
I never even fretted
I did not bat an eyelid
I never even flinched
But to survive in my world
You definitely could not cringe
Survival of the fittest
A dog eat dog world
Where the weak get picked on in less than a minute
I wish I could have protected you
But nobody showed me how
For this is what I am accustomed to
Believe me I am not proud
I regretted I was not bolder
That I did not scream and shout
Because these guilt ridden voices seem so loud

Changing

When someone says "you have changed" they hate it
Not because you actually have but because they never can and cannot stand it
Changing is growing
Staying the same is dying
Both are a slow process
One is a blessing
The other is a stressing

Rose Tinted Glasses

Yes I miss you
Even though you are no good for me
But those rose tinted glasses slipped off slowly
And I started to see things a little more clearly
So when he holds my hand
When he strokes my face
When we go out to our favourite place
Hopefully you can finally realise
Yes you have been replaced

Demons in the Dark

I have so many demons locked away
That I cannot recognise which one creeps out to play
The more I try to suppress them
The more it seems I fed them
I thought the only way to starve them was to keep them in the dark
But it turned out they grew stronger and left me with unwanted scars and marks
They have been living with me now for about 12 years
I have given them a nice home in my mental dome
Which is why they will not leave me alone

Delicious Dear

I have tried reaching out to you so many times
Even in my personal poetic rhymes
I have tried to tell you how I feel
I am the one with the rough end of this deal
I have tried to show you how much I care
But take it in? You would not dare
I am telling you I am lonely and need you here
But you brush it off like you did not hear
We all have our own fears my dark delicious dear
But mine heighten when you are not near

Creeping

I have tried running away from you for so long
That I did not stop to realise what I was doing was so wrong
I could not let myself believe anything you ever told me
But when I sat and thought about it
I could feel everything you ever showed me
I would always come back to you wanting more
Then creep out slowly through the front door
No matter how many times I try to leave you
No matter how many times you take me back
You are and will always be my delicious vicious cycle
And my happy downward spiral

Temporary Fix

He does not get me like you do
But he gets me when I cannot get to you
He does not make me feel like you do
But close enough to make me forget my feelings for you
I know it is only a temporary fix until I deal with my feelings and thoughts for you
But until then he is my glue and rubber
Slowly sticking me back together and erasing my memories of you

Are You Worth It?

If I have to tell you I am worth it
Then you are not worth my time
For I am a dollar and you are a dime
If I have to keep showing you that I care
And you blow it away like air
Then I can and will no longer care
If you cannot feel anything from my touch, embrace or the smile I bring to your face
Then all the above is not worthwhile and I will not apologise for being hostile

My Song

Mind your own
While I do my own
Just because you think it is wrong
Does not actually make it wrong
I will hum along to my own sweet song
While you sit and listen to mine
Because in my world
This is a solo and I am doing just fine
A closed set no room for trios or duets
Do not be upset
Go and learn a song of your own

My Blessing

She crept into my heart
How I do not know
She soothed my soul
And filled that hole
She captivated my thoughts
And fascinated my mind
The scary thing is
She did not even have to try
But I never wanted this
I was not ready
But it felt like bliss
Like our souls were kissing
I did not even realise that this is what I was missing
Until I got a taste of her
I realised she was my blessing

Why I Let Her Go

I let him have her
I did not even put up a fight
I know you think I'm crazy
But for once I did what was right
She wanted me
But needed him
He is not like me
He is pretty dim
She says it is easy with him
But he does not make her feel at ease
He likes to please her
Which is what she needs
I will always love her
More than she will ever know
Which is why I made the hardest decision
Which is why I let her go

Substitution

Substitute:
A person or thing acting or serving in place of another.
You can substitute soya milk for dairy
Dried herbs for fresh
But when it comes down to that special feeling you get with that one person
Nothing will ever compare to your version of heavenly pleasure you have right there

Call My Bluff

My love for you was hot like fire
I would have done anything you wished for and desired
But when you crossed me I became colder than ice
I cut you off like you were no sacrifice
You should be flattered
Because it means you once meant the world to me
Now you mean absolutely nothing
Try me and see if I am bluffing

Remember and Recognise

Remember when you pushed me away?
He pulled me closer.
Remember when you tried to pull the wool over my eyes?
He opened them and made me see things more clearer.
Remember when you said you were busy?
So was he but he always made time for me.
Remember when you made me feel like I was crazy?
He made me feel at peace.
Remember the anxious knots you made me feel?
He replaced them with butterflies.
Remember that stupid little girl who was in love with you?
His love tuned her into a strong woman who did not want you anymore.
I am sure you remember her
But you definitely will not recognise me anymore.

Insecurity vs Intuition

Why does this feel like I am never going to see, touch or taste you again?
Is it my insecurities going down memory lane
Or my intuition trying to tell my brain?
The worst goodbyes are the ones never said
They are the ones that really mess up your head
If I am right please take the memories with you
They hurt too much to reminisce of you
I can block them out without a doubt
Just when you leave
Please do not take my heart with you

The Heartbreaker

I knew you were a heartbreaker
But this is not the way I thought you would have broken mine
I knew you were a heartbreaker
But I thought we were doing more than just fine
I knew you were a heartbreaker
But because you thought I broke yours
That does not excuse the fact that you broke mine
It might have been unintentional
To protect your heart from breaking
But I was not the one you needed protecting from
It was from yourself
Now look what we have become
Friends that turned into lovers
Lovers that turned into strangers
With the heartbreaker back on track
And me with a heart full of cracks

Secret Treasure

It was a moment of madness
Because of my sadness
That I fell for you
It was my vulnerability
It was your consistency
That made me open up to you
It was my addiction to the pleasure you showed and made me feel
That made you my all-time secret treasure
Because there was no pressure
It was all just for leisure
But now I have fallen for you
Which I was not supposed to do

Wanting More

When I bumped into you that day
I wish I had more stupid conversation and thought of something to say
I wish I had the courage to touch you
Just a little stroke
But I acted like a shy kid
What a joke!
We kissed goodbye on the cheeks
But I wished it was on your lips
Or maybe even grabbed your hips
Instead just a tiny worthless catch up
Which has left me wanting a close up
Because that definitely was not enough

He vs Me

I never realised what love was until I lost her
I never realised how much I needed her until she did not need me anymore
I never realised how beautiful she was until I saw the way he made her smile
I never realised what loss was until she did not want me anymore
I never realised what heartbreak was until she told me she loved him and not me anymore
But she was my cure…
And I never truly knew the meaning of "too little too late"
Until I realised there goes my soul mate

Love Triangle

How can I break her heart without breaking mine?
If I stay she will be ok
If I stay I will not be ok
How can I stay and not break her heart?
If I do not leave her I break hers and mine

Lovers vs Fighters

Yes I am your lover
But I will not fight for you
For what wants to love me
I do not have to fight for

The Beautiful Beast

I wish I knew
I wish I might
Get an insight
Of that dark and dangerous mind
To unleash and get under
That beautiful beast
To see if it has a heart
To see if it actually beats
I wish I knew
I wish I might
Actually like it in that mind
And stay there for all my nights
To undo and unlock
That rage that has been caged
To calm and caress
That beauty that lies beneath
I wish I knew
I wish I might
To be able to intensify and show the light
To excite the passion and ignite
I wish I knew
I wish I might

Not Yet

I am not ready for you to leave me
I am not ready for you to walk away
We push and pull at each other through our highs and lows
Please just stay one more day
I cannot bear to watch you walk away
For every time you do
I lose a piece of me to you
A piece I cannot get back
A piece that forms another crack
I am not ready for you to leave me
Please come back

Sink or Swim

Just like a wreckage in the sea
We are starting to drift away slowly
The more I try to swim to you
The more the sea pulls me away from you
I am holding onto a little piece of what is left of our boat
A little piece of hope
Trying my hardest to keep a float
Wondering if I let go
Will I sink or swim?

Wake Up

I would have done anything and everything for you
I even gave up my home, family and friends for you
I really thought you had my back
I thought we were so tight
That we never had any cracks
I thought we were on the same team
Just you and me
But in reality it all feels like a really bad dream
One that I do not know if I can ever wake from

Do You? I Do

Do you love me?
I do not know
Do you want me?
I think so
Do you need me?
Undoubtedly
Can you live without me?
……..
I do not even want to try

Goodbye

I have to do what is best for me
So now I have to leave
I have to do what is best for me
And keep you away from me
I have to do the right thing
Even though it is hard for me
I have to do the right thing
Even if it kills me

Colours of the Ice Queen

Do you really think I do not break?
I think you like to push me to see if I am real
To see how much I can take
You may think I am an ice queen
But I do actually feel and do break
Into millions of pieces every night
It can be a sore sight
But to show you?
I never will and never might
When the morning comes I see the light
It takes all my might to be alright
Just remember not everything you see is black and white

Converse

I wish I knew why you went so cold
I wish you could be so bold
I wish you would communicate
Maybe even articulate and educate

My Salvation

I am not quiet because I have nothing to say
I am quiet because I love to watch you when you have something to say
The way your lips move and the shapes they make
There is certain parts that they awake
The way your eyes sparkle
The dimple in your chin
When you make that ever so sexy grin
You are my salvation
I am lost in translation
Words cannot express what I want to say

What Magic Can Do

He looked at her like she was magic
She sparkled because he made her believe it

Boy to a Man

I want to go back to the beginning
From the start where you always had my heart
Two young teenagers
Who were just strangers
Back then I always thought I was smart
But as we grew up together
I realised it was you who was actually smart…
Intelligent, beautiful and caring
You would always wear on your sleeve
That ever so genuine heart
The day I became a man from a boy
Was when I broke it
Not because that made me tough or hard
But when I realised that I lost you
My whole life flashed before me
When you put up your guard
The rage of losing you
The thought of never seeing you or feeling your touch really aged my soul
It took me to a low place
That I had to depart
I broke it down with everything I had inside me
Bit by bit
Scar by scar
And now I am your physical and emotional guard
When you forgave me and welcomed me with open arms
I swore I would never let you see a day or night with harm
Full term and long term
You will always have my heart
From the day I met you
Until God or whatever makes me depart

Today's Generation

Seriously…do you not have any game?
Nowadays you guys are so lame
I cannot really blame you
Well I can a bit
From these so called women
That give it up in just one hit
Each to their own I suppose
I know should not judge
But it is going to take a lot more for me to budge
In this day and age all it takes is a bit of texting
Then straight away people are sexing
People are so thirsty
What happened to actually getting to know someone firstly?
Conversing and reserving
Actually get turned on by their mind
Instead of hitting it and dispersing

I Wish

I wish you would let me kiss you
So you could feel how much I miss you
But you keep telling me you do not know where my lips have been
I keep telling you they have been all over and under you a thousand times in my dreams
I wish you would let me hold you
So you can remember how it felt to be in my embrace
But that look on your face is so damn cold
I know you want to you are just acting proud and bold

Undo the Blindfold

Of course it hurt when I lost you
But the you I lost was not the you I knew
Maybe it was I cannot be sure
They say love is blind and we all know it can be unkind
But I am ready to take the blindfold off to see what I can find

Lying in Bed

I lay in my bed and think of all the things I could say to you
I lay in my bed and think of all the things I could do with you
I lay in my bed and remember how it felt to lie next to you
I lay in my bed and wish I was wrapped around you
But when I wake up the next day
I push it all to a certain part of my brain
The part that tries to forget
The part that is filed under “upset” and “reset”
I make it through the day
But not at night when I lay
The day is easy
It seems so bright
The night is hard
It fills me with fright

Love vs Hate

I do not love to hate you
Quite the opposite
I hate it that I love you

Heart vs Head

There will always be a certain smile that I have that only you can bring
There will always be a secret song to my soul that only you can sing
There will always be a place in my mind that only you can get and find
For in that moment we truly are aligned
There will always be a place in my heart that is still waiting for you
There will always be a piece of my heart that only belongs to you
But I will not let my heart rule my head this time
Which is why only a piece of it belongs to you

He & Her

I had to let her go
I would hurt her less this way
I had to walk away
He never wanted me anyway
I wanted her more than ever before
I got tired of waiting for him to walk through my door
I purposely made her feel like she was not enough
He made me feel like I was not the one
I wished her well even though it felt like hell
He let me go and released me from his spell

Regret

I do not regret always being there for you
I do not even regret being loyal to you
I definitely do not regret the nights I gave myself up to you
But when there is nobody around
When it all falls down
You will regret that I am not there for you

I'd Like To

I would like to be able to say I love you
But I hate that phrase
I have heard it so many times
Like it was just a phase

Past Lives

You must be my soul mate from a past life
My body feels like it is remembering your touch, sensation and all it arised
You must be my soul mate from a past life
Because nothing hurts as much as you do
Not even if you were to stab me with a knife
We must be soul mates from a past life
You were my husband and I was your wife
You are my soul mate
I will go through all my nine lives
For you to remember my touch, sensation and all it arised

Him & Her

I wish you felt for me as half as you do for her
I wish I felt for him as half as I do for you
I wish you would remember me
As bad as I am trying to forget you
I wish you felt for me as half as you do for her
Then I would not be feeling so foolish
Waiting for you at my door
For having these feelings leaves me crying on the floor

Let's Go Back

I miss you
I really do
I want to call you up and just tell you
But I will not
I cannot
Not because of my pride
Let's face it that went out the window when I let a lot slide
I will not because I will not be able to handle it when you say it back
Because if you really missed me why will you not take me back?
Back to the days when it felt good
Back to the way it was just us two

Will & Why

Why is the beginning always the hardest?
Like your first day at school
Will I make any friends, will they think I am cool?
First day at a new job
Will my boss like me or will he be a completer knob?
First date with your crush
Will it go well or will I say something awkward and blush?
Why are we always over analysing and over thinking instead of just enjoying the moment and being satisfied?
Why do we always need to know the answers right there and then instead of just letting it grow and beautifully begin?

Where to Start

There are so many things I want to say to you
That nothing actually comes out
The end, the beginning and the middle are all mixed up
I would not know where to start from or what to finish with and what to leave out
Scared of saying too much and not enough
Scared of you not getting it at all and being left feeling numb
Being misunderstood and misjudged
Do I just spurt it all out and hope you make sense of it and risk it all sounding like junk?

Onwards and Upwards

I gave it everything I had
It took everything I had
With all the strength I gave
I am taking it back
I am giving it all to me
Back to fix my cracks
I am my healer
Just me
With the same strength I gave not to give up
I am counting my blessings
Even my lessons
Because once you have been so far down
The only way left is up

Loving & Leaving

I need some time out
Time away from you
I need to leave us
But I do not want to leave you
I have gotten in too deep
That I cannot see any light shining through
I do not know how to be friends with someone
When there is not a me and you
I do not know how to handle it
Do I throw in the towel, walk away and admit defeat?
Or do I put on a brave heart and face and pretend that I am fine with this distant space?
I have never experienced this much pain from walking away
I have never experienced leaving the one I am in love with to find better days
I have always been the one to leave
When I know it is done
I know this will be better for me in the long run
But I have never left someone who is my loved one

Writing the Unwritten

How can I write about love when I have forgotten how it feels?
How can I write about hope when it has not helped me heal?
How can I write about happy endings when all I have ever known is self-depending?
How can I write about you when you are so overdue?
I can write about the beginning and the middle…
But how can I write about the ending when it is still a riddle?

Time and Crime

We always loved each other
Like spiritually and sexually connected lovers
Our only crime was
It was never at the same time

Can the Unfixable be Fixed?

I felt asphyxiated
Lack of love and care
It made me do things
Out of despair
I thought I found my crucifix
But you were not no Jesus
I became fixated on you
Around you I was nervous
I fixed myself around you
Fastened my legs securely around your heavenly body and waist
You became my fix
Around you my heart always raced
I am left with infixed memories in my mind
Things I should have never seen
That in that moment I wish I was blind
I do not think that they will ever hide
They like to stay there even though they are never kind
Through it all I have become transfixed
Wondering if what I am left with can be fixed
Wondering what will be my next fix
Wondering can the unfixable be fixed

The Controller

You make me feel like I am bipolar
One day so high
That every day is filled with blue skies
The next day it is filled with lies and cries that I could not really care if I died
You make me feel like I am peculiar
For asking of you the simplest things like respect, love and honesty
Which is always the best policy
But for you I think it is not
I hate the fact that you are my controller
When all I ever wanted was a sympathetic and soothing shoulder
I thought I pulled out a king instead it was a joker
You may think you have fooled me but clearly you have not
I am a warrior
Defeat me?
You will not

The Dome

Why do I love the darkness so much?
Why do I love the taste of bittersweet on my tongue?
Why am I more comfortable in the shadows than in the light?
Why do I feel at peace at night?
Why does pain feel like my second home?
Why do I like it in this doom and gloomy dome?

The Rebel vs The Cause

You make feel alive
Even though you are smoothly killing me
You make me feel complete
Even though you are taking pieces of me
You make me feel innocent
Even though you are my guilty pleasure
You make me feel like I am in heaven
Even though my sins will send me to hell
You make me feel like I am under a magical spell
Even though I know this is not going to end well
I am the rebel
You are my cause
I need to find a get out clause

Choices

Yes I am loyal
Yes I am kind
Yes I am real
And feel a lot of the time
But that is just how things work in my mind
This is the way I choose to be
But I am not confused
Just like the yin and yang of life
I know there is different types of walks of life
After all this is real life
Not everybody is from the same way of life
I am not saying my life is any better
But I have never been a quitter
I will not let real life change me
Or try to rearrange me
Yes I am loyal
Yes I am kind
Yes I am real
And feel a lot of the time
But that is just the way I chose to live my life

Constant Hunger

He only wanted a taste of her
Because he knew if he had all of her
He would be the one that could not satisfy and fulfil her hunger
So he would rather taste her coating
Than be eaten up by her core
Because when she would digest him fully
She would throw him up and spit him out on the floor
So he would rather worship her from a far
Than look up at her on his knees from the floor

Fight vs Fear

Do not be scared of me
Please…
What harm could I actually do?
Make you feel
Make you heal
Is that really such a big deal?
Do not be scared of you?
Please…
What good could you actually do?
Make me weak
Make me vulnerable
These things I do not want to feel
Do not be scared
Please…
I am on my knees
Let me in
Under your skin
I am scared
Please…
I am on my knees
Just go
My heart left me a long time ago

Emotional Millionaires

I am lying in my bed
With thoughts of you running through my head
Wishing you were here instead
Thinking of you lying beside me
On our sides
Just looking at each other
Completely naked with nothing to hide
No fronting
Just smiling
Thinking
For once could this actually be worthwhile?
It does not feel awkward
It feels like we are at ease
And our gift to each other
Is the feeling of peace
To calm our fears
To stop our tears
To forget all our past affairs
To feel like emotional millionaires

Fixation

We waste so much time trying to fix people
When in fact the only person that can fix them is themselves
Let it go
Otherwise the only person you will be needing to fix is yourself

Let Her Go

She scared him
But not in an aggressive or intimidating way
She scared him because she was the total opposite
Gentle, calming, soothing and silent
She scared him because she did not need to do much at all and she still pleased his heart and soul
This scared him right down to his bones
For he thought if she had this much impact on him by not doing much
Imagine what she could do to him if really let her in
She scared him
So he walked away

Fear Less to be Fearless

To the emotionally challenged:
It is a shame you did not let their love in because you were scared
It is a shame you did not give them a chance because who knows?
You could have been something great
It is a shame that you do not give as much as they do instead you just take
It is a shame because you as a person could be someone great
It is a shame because you will always be looking for that missing piece which actually is inside of you
It is a shame you always go with the easy option because it is exactly that
It is a shame when you will look back at all your past opportunities and realise it is a shame your fears stopped you from being someone fearless and great, with that one person who was fearless and great, being fearless and great with somebody else who is fearless and great.
It is a shame you cannot fear less to be great

Talking to a Stranger

Where are you?
I do not know how much more I can take without you
It is crazy longing for you
When I do not even know who you are
I do not know what you look like
Let alone taste, smell or even sound like
Yet I still crave for and need you
But we must be alike
Missing one and another
Thinking the same about each other
I cannot bear to have to meet another if it is not you
I am scared I will give up from disappointment
Then miss my date with fate

Sweet Dreams?

We all have certain rules we live our lives by
But do they actually help you sleep at night?
Can you close your eyes, rest your head on that pillow
And turn off your conscience mind?

Affections and Effects

We all need to travel a lot more and work a lot less
I would rather get out of the country than go out every night to forget my stress
To see a beautiful sun rise and set
With a magical moonlight perfect reflect
To reconnect with my soul
To collect my thoughts
To enjoy this amazing world's affects of the effects

With You When I Am Not

I might not be with you tonight
But I will be wearing the smile you left me with tonight
I might not be able to touch you tonight
But I will be touching the places you last kissed me on tonight
I might not be able to see you tonight
But I will be seeing you in my wildest dreams tonight
Until we meet again
I will slowly but sweetly go insane
With thoughts of you tantalising and teasing my brain

Don’ts and Won’ts

That empty space on my bed misses you
But I do not
That red dress I wore when we went to our favourite place misses you
But I do not
That kitchen table we made dinners on misses you
But I do not
That sofa we used to spend Sundays on curled up together misses you
But I do not
Even my lips and hips miss you
But I do not
If I keep telling myself I do not
Then maybe I actually will not

Which Way?

I cannot explain why I feel anxious whenever you leave me
Isi it my intuition trying to tell me something or my insecurities?
If you want this to terminate and just be friends then please say
We can go our separate ways
If this is all in my head
Then take my hand and lead the way

Just One

Nobody is perfect
Not even me
Everybody comes with a past
Some who would like to forget about it fast
I am just looking for that one person to build a future with
That can last

Pick Me!

For once I want someone to choose me
I want to be the one they are afraid of losing
I want to be the one they bend over backwards for to please
The one if they do not hear from they do not feel at ease
The one to make someone else feel at peace
To be their missing piece
To increase the smile on their face when they see me
My presence to mean just as much as my absence
For once…Please

The Sorry You Never Got

I am sorry you met me
I am sorry I made you smile inside
I am sorry I made you get lost in the moment with me
I am sorry for leading you on when I knew you would fall for me
I am sorry that was my plan all along to make you want me because of my own insecurities, my own selfish ways for you to feed my ego
What I am most sorry for is that when I knew I had won and got what I wanted to make myself feel good again
I walked away
I am sorry I am sorry

Time's Up

I wasted so much time
Like you were just a part time
Initially you were just meant to be a one time
But in the mean time
You became my high time
Eventually I became your low time
I finally did it though
I left
And you were right…
You were not there like you said would not be
I wish I could rewrite it above all
To have noticed that you meant it when you said
"I would have given you it all"

Anthology

I still love you…
But what hurts the most is that I know you still do too
Which is why one night with you
Feels like heaven and hell
You ignite every one of my bodily cells
With you next to me
Forget poetry
I could write a novel with a trilogy

I Need Him

I need him
Because when I am with him I forget about you
But honestly I do not want him
I want you
The difference is
I do not need you
Like I need him
And I do not want him
Like I want you

Bullet Proof Vest

Do not dare call me heartless
Just because I have finally learnt how to use it less
After all…
I learnt from the best
You put me through so many tests
That now I wear an invisible bullet proof vest
You would not even be able to hear my heartbeat
If you placed your head on my chest
This was all so hard for me to digest
For everything I had I did invest
But your greatest pain
Is your greatest teacher
So for that I am blessed

The Right Thing

I saw you today
Not sure if you saw me though
I wanted to walk right up to you and give you a hug
But I did not and that my friend was tough
After all I was the one who chose to walk away
And told you stay away
Even if it was the right decision that I made
The pain I felt could never be man made
For the love I have for you had not gone away
For the love I have for you could never be misplaced
For it all came back to me today

Can We?

Can we just skip this whole fronting part?
The part where you play it cool because you do not want to look like a fool
The part where you hold back because you have lost track of how many times it did not work before
The part where you stop yourself from calling because you are scared of falling
Can we just skip this part and show me if your heart is real?

Soul Kiss

A kiss is just a kiss until it is the kind of kiss you have been missing
The kind of kiss that was buried deep in your abyss
That now is filled with butterflies and bliss
A soul type kiss

Destruction

We destroy each other when we are together and we destroy ourselves when we are apart
Which is better…
To be destroyed in your presence or absence?
Either way you will always play a magnificent part

Attraction vs Connection

Maybe we are destined to only be friends and that is why we kept getting it wrong
Maybe we are destined to be in each other lives but not how we want
Maybe we got our attraction for each other confused with our connection for each other and that is where we went wrong

Wherever Blessed

Wherever I travel to near or far
Wherever my feet can take me
Wherever I can see the stars
Wherever I lay my head
The memories will rest in my heart
Wherever I go to
I am blessed by far

Traveller's Dream

As long as I am free to travel
Travelling will always set me free
I want a passport full of memories
From every place I will see
I want a suitcase of experience
That I can unpack anywhere and gratefully reminisce

Admit

Sometimes I want to scream out loud
"I miss you and think about you every god damn day"
Just so maybe the thought of you could go away
They say the first step to overcoming your addiction is admitting you have a problem
So here it goes…
I miss you and think about you every god damn day

Memories

Don't you hate it when you make a mental note NOT to forget something but you always do?
I wish I could do that with you

Give vs Take

The story of us
I gave too much
You took too much
The story of my life

Dream vs Nightmare

Which is the dream and which is the nightmare?
Loving you in my sleep
Or waking up alone?

One Day

There is not one day I do not think about you
It might not be all day, half a day or even an hour
But it is definitely everyday even if it is for a minute
My thoughts you empower
There is not one day I do not regret the way things have turned out
For if I stayed a day longer any self-respect I had left you would have devoured
But one day I will stop thinking of you and release myself from this mental tower
For my head and heart you will not over power

First Crush

You are soft on the eye
I think you are lush
When you smile my way
I get a rush
But when I am without you
When you leave my side
That is when I know the meaning of crush

Thank You

You made it easy for me to walk away
Because when I needed you, you were never there anyway
You made me accustomed to being on my own
That walking away did not scare me of being alone

Lost vs Found

I take the long way home in hopes I might see you
In hopes we will pass each other
In hopes the universe will give us at least three seconds of seeing each other
For in those three seconds
I am home
That is the thing about being lost
You hope you will be found

X-Ray

I wish my heart could break like my bones
So you could see the breaks and the fractures
Then maybe you would understand my pain
Understand why I cannot ever walk the same way again

Types of Love

In all my lifetimes that I have lived
I have learnt that we all love differently
It never meant I was never loved
I was loved secretly, sensually, sweetly and scarily
Love is love

The Importance of a Pillow

You get to hold your human pillow
I get to hold a pillow of sorrow
You do not know how lucky you are
When you do not have to sleep alone

The Last Night

I know I said the last night would be the last night
But last night I spent with you
I thought if I closed my eyes
I could close my heart too

Sensitive vs Numb

I have never been afraid of being sensitive
But I am afraid I am becoming numb

Grief

My heart grieves for me
As much I grieve for you

Then vs Now

I never used to smoke until the day you left
Now I only smoke your brand to feel you on my lips again
I never used to drink until the day you left
Now only drink your brand of whiskey to feel you in my heart again
I do not do much since you left
Because I do not want to feel again

Wanting

He wanted to be with her
But he was not strong enough
He was not afraid of his past
But afraid of what she would have thought of it
He wanted to know what it would feel like to touch her soft skin
Instead he settled to watch it glow in the sun
He wanted to know what her lips tasted like
He so wanted to be that coffee in her cup
Come to think of it who ever came near her would never come close enough
And he was afraid he would not be good enough

Hope

My hope is what kept us together in the beginning
My hope is what made me fall apart in the end
That is the thing about hope
She is like a double edged sword
She can bring your life up
She can also leave you bleeding on the floor

Rarity & Repair

Her smile can be innocent yet naughty
The same as her stare, either one I do not care
For they both make me feel something rare
She makes me want to lay myself bare
When she kisses me she does repair
When I am curled up in her lair
Try to leave her?
I do not dare

Too Tired

I am too tired to pretend I am strong
I am too tired to pretend you did not do anything wrong
So please save all the BS
Take all your mess with you
I am too tired to walk you out
You know where the front door is
Be gone and stay gone

Dragon and Demons

We all have addictions
Mine are blades, bottles and blunts
Blades to cut open and bleed
To see if I actually have anything left under my skin
Bottles to feel something burn
To stop the bitter cold in my heart
Blunts to smoke it all away, fly away
To forget and become numb
That is the thing about addictions
You keep chasing the dragon
But when they are over the dragon and the demons chase you

The Walking Dead

Confessions of the walking dead:
You can love me but you cannot hurt me
For I am already dead

Stand Still vs Move On

How am I supposed to move on
When all I see is you moving on without me?

I Pick Me!

I always wanted you to pick me
Like a child in class or a player for a team
No matter how much my eyes would gleam
Or I would scream "PICK ME!"
But you never did
Month after month, year after year
Through all my tears
No matter how much I adhered
But you never did
You never saw or maybe even chose to ignore the potential in me
But eventually I found someone who did
I finally realised my potential and worth
I picked me

The Heart Collector

The heart collector likes to collect hearts
And does it with such an art
Makes you voluntarily land in the jar
Not touching you but never being too far
Watches you closely through the glass
While your little heart flutters trying to breathe
He mutters
"Do not worry the pain will not last"
The heart collector
Easy to fall for but hard to catch
Closes the lid on his heart collection
Places the jar on the shelf
Walks away
Game, set and match

Drunk vs Sober

Do you ever think about me?
When you are drunk full of regrets and mistakes
Full of what could have beens while you are filling up another glass
When you have managed to crawl into bed with you head spinning of past images of us making love and laughing
When you are ready to throw up
Wishing I was there to calm you
When you are smoking flying high
Leaving all of what is underneath you
Meeting me in night dreams to forget the nightmares that taunt you
Do you ever think if I still think of you while I am sober without you?

Fear My Dear

Why are we so certain that someone likes us when we do not like them
But when we like someone we are so uncertain they like us?
Fear my dear

Apparent Parenting

I am sure you have made mistakes in your life
As I am sure your child will too
But the unconditional love you proclaim
Comes with terms and conditions because you have your own unrealistic ambitions
If they are not met there are cold cut dismissions
It has become apparent that just because you are a parent
Sometimes…
Blood is not always thicker than water

Save You vs Save Me

Some men are heroes but not the romantic types
Not like the ones who sweep you off your feet with flowers and sweet nothings to save you
But the ones who will pull away and cut you off to protect you
To keep you at a distance
To keep you away from harm and pain
Who seem to be faraway but are watching you closely
Heroes are self-sacrificing
But really who are they trying to save?

It's Not Me, It's You

It is not you, it is me
You are right
But it was only until I left I believed it
It was you, not me

With You vs Without You

I do not have the time or patience to argue anymore
We can either talk about the problem, resolve it and move on
Or not talk and move on our separate ways
Either way I am moving on with or without you

Forgotten How To Feel

She was only ever wanted for the way she looked and made them feel
That she forgot how it felt to feel
But when he made her smile she was not sure if it was for his satisfaction or hers
She was not sure if it or he was real

Human Mirrors

What you see in me is a reflection of you
If you do not like what the image is showing you
Maybe it is time to start self-reflecting and stop dejecting

Changing vs Choosing

What happens to you is not because of who you are
It is because it is life
Thankfully life is forever changing as so are you
You make the choice if it is for good or bad
You are the choice and the reason

My Crazy vs Your Crazy

You all think I am crazy because I care too much
Because I feel too much
I think you are all crazy because you do not care or feel enough
Maybe I am, maybe I am not
But I would rather feel something than nothing at all

Ego vs Pride

She said no to me so I threw her away
Disregarded her feelings and thoughts as to why she told me no
I only thought about my feelings and my thoughts as to why she told me no
Only me
Only my ego
But the craziest thing happened
Even though she stood up for herself
Even though she stood up to me
It made me want her more
That is the thing about ego and pride
It can make you strong
It can make you wrong
But you cannot be both at the same time
So I stayed strong and never spoke to her again
I stayed wrong and longed for her with my head secretly held down in shame

Bitter vs Sweet

He crept into my bed again last night
The same way he crept into my mind
He covered me with his soft silky skin
Which woke up all of my desires within
I could smell him before he entered
That's what caused me to stir
But until he touched me with that firm recognisable grip
He looked just like a blur
He opened my mouth
Along with my heart and soul
Then looked deep in my eyes
Which made me long for more
For being next to him never felt like a chore
I could feel he adored me
From how hungry he was
As he slammed against the door
And as I looked up
I was actually on the floor
For he was my bitter sweet dream
From which I needed a cure

Invisible Tattoo

I have to go soon
I'm starting to become un immune to you
I have to go soon
I'm starting to fall for your mesmerizing tune
But when I do
You will be my invisible tattoo
Full of ink stained into my skin and bruised
Out of all of them I would still choose you
For you are my favourite muse

Loved vs Unloved

Why cannot anyone understand?
All I need and want is a loving hand
To have and to hold
To protect me and be bold
To set a standard for people I allow in my life
To protect me from this world that is full of strife's
I know I hardly know you
Or remember when you walked out
It might not even bother you
Or cause you any doubt
That the first person I should have known and loved
Is the first person who made me feel uninvolved and unloved

Follow You

All it took was one glance
When I saw you that night
Took the chance
And asked you to dance
All it took was one smile from you
And I knew I would travel miles to see you
All it took was one three letter word
When you made me the happiest man on this earth
All it took was the birth of our children to make us complete
And truly know my worth
All it took was you in that hospital bed
And I immediately knew that I wished it was me instead
When you died that morning
My effortlessly beautiful darling
Without any warning
You did not just take a piece of me with you
You took every last bit of my breath
And I instantly knew
I wanted to follow you

His Beauty and Her Beast

She was his beauty
And he was a beast
He lived in the night
Where he loved to feast
He would stand in the shadows
And watch his prey
While his hunger for her
Could not be delayed
He craved for her
Like he had not eaten for days
He wanted to taste her
And take her away
He knew if she saw him for what he actually was
She would run with fear as fast as she could
So he stands in the dark
And secretly claims her
Watching and protecting his beauty forever

Free Yourself

Sometimes you have to go back
To be able to move forward
You need that clarification
To find a satisfactory destination
It might be better the second time round
But unfortunately life isn't a fairground
Not everything is black and white
Yes or no
Wrong or right
If you need to go back then do it
Sometimes you need to crack and split open
To be filled with emotion
Don't forget you are only human
Once you have received your answers and you are at peace
Then you are ready to close that door and be free

Cry

When I see you cry
Please do not go shy
For that is when you are most beautiful and sensational
Real, raw and emotional
The way your eyes sparkle when your tears are near
Your lips plump up and your cheeks go red
That is when I so want to put you to bed
I want to stroke your hair
I want to caress your cheeks
I want to pull you closer so you do not feel weak
You can always have my shoulder to cry on and hand to hold
For when this world gets cold
You will always have me to rely on

Tears & Fears

She turned to him and asked
With tears and fears falling down her face
"Would you want me au naturelle?"
He turned and said to her smiling
"Of course my dear, for that is when I love you the most."

What If

If I was to die tomorrow would you be sad?
Would you regret the chances you never took but had?
Would you sit and reminisce or block me out like I did not exist?
Would you keep your feelings a secret like you always did or tell the world you loved me but was just too damn scared?
Would you have wished you dared?
Would you sit and think about what we could have shared and laid yourself bare?
Or would you carry on like you never cared?

A Lost Cause

I want you
But I do not want your world
I want you
But I do not want to be your girl
I love you
For all the good I see
I love you
For when we are together we can just be
I have tried to save you
To make you see the light
But you love it in your twisted life
I have tried to save you
But then I realised
It is how you are programmed so I gave up this fight
You are already comfortably lost
Sadly your beautiful soul was the cost
I will always be here for you looking in
And dream of what we could have been

Thank You

You made it easy for me to walk away
Because when I needed you
You were never there anyway
You had me accustomed to being on my own
That walking away did not scare me of being alone
I did not want your gifts, money or holidays
I wanted your time and affection
All the things that you cannot pay
You made me realise how it should not be and feel
That what I thought we had was not the real deal
But I would like to thank you, you should thank yourself too
For you gave me the strength to walk away
I think we both know it was well over due

I Am

I am going to break you down into loads of pieces until we get down to your core
Then I am going to fix you back up stronger than before
We are going to argue until you hate me
Then you will love me because I made you see sides to you more clearly
I am going to bring you calmness and make you feel at peace
Where all you ever felt was anger and insecure
I will always be here with you even when you think I am not
Just look deep inside you when you feel that knot
Open your eyes and see
I am you and you are me

Expression vs Repression

To the un-expressionist words can mean so much
To the expressionist silence can mean just as much
But one thing they both have in common
Is that they crave for that ever so soft and sensual touch
Which they both use as their crutch
To cling to and to clutch to
This can never be too much
For the un-expressionist and the expressionist feel so much

My Curse vs My Cure

You are my curse as well as my cure
For both I feel very pure
You are my cure as well as my curse
For both I need a nurse
You have my heart as well as my scars
For you gave meaning to both
I cannot live with you
I cannot live without you
So what am I to do?
Live a day of joy and bliss
Or live a night in the darkest abyss?
With one hand you can save me
With the other you kill me
Either way please do not leave me
Either way please do not hate me
Either way please just love me

Asleep vs Awake

You ask me how can I can be so real and raw?
I ask you how can you be so fake, is it not tiring and a bore?
You ask me am I not scared of looking dumb?
I ask you are you not scared of feeling numb?
It is a shame that you would rather be shallow than deep
It is a shame you are afraid to speak
To speak of things that really matter
To speak of things that make your whole world scream, shine and shatter
You ask me why would I want to feel these things?
I ask you would you not rather feel than sleep?
Be asleep to the things that can make you feel alive
Be asleep to the things that can take you down to a sweet death dive

Temporary vs Permanent

I wish I could take away the pain for you
I really do
I wish I could show you the future
So you could have a clue
To see it will get better
In time it always does
Because just like happiness and sadness
Nothing lasts forever
So follow your heart and follow your soul
For in the end my darling
This should be your only goal
It might be wrong but it could be right
For this is what is going to help you sleep at night

I am vs I am not

I am not the kind of girl to get her bits out for some likes
I am not the kind of girl to be out with a different guy every night
I am the kind of girl who prefers quality over quantity
I am the kind of girl who prefers to stay in and write
Call me boring call me lame
But I would rather be different than the same
Each to their own
Even though there are so many clones
For in this generations society
Where there is so much variety
People are always looking for better
But to me they are all just like blank letters
I would rather be alone

Home Alone

She was like a little island all on her own
Private yet peaceful
Secluded yet sensational
You could see the sun rise in her eyes when she smiled
You could see the sun set in her eyes when she cried
She was too beautiful to be on her own
People would always come and people would always go
But nobody would actually set up home

Silence vs Storm

I bend but I do not break
I give but I do not take
I am not perfect I make mistakes
I am only human I do ache
This does not shake me
It only makes me
Pull me push me
Like a storm I will awake

I Will Be Me

I know I am not the person I want to be yet
But I am trying to be step by step
I know it will not happen overnight
My journey is going to be a fright
Fretting and fighting with myself
Over past and future decisions I have made and will make every night
But I know who I want to be and for me that is a start
To follow my head and to follow my heart
Now is a fresh start
Now is a better time than any to be who I truly want
I need to please me
I know it is not going to be easy
But it is harder not being who I want to be

Fit In vs Stand Out

You are so busy trying to fit into the next designer dress or suit
That you have forgotten it is more important to stand out and not follow suit
Do your own thing and be proud
You do not need everybody's acceptance you are allowed
Allowed to be you
Allowed to be free
I feel sorry for you if you do not agree

Beautiful vs Burdened

His hands were beautiful but burdened
Beautiful for what he could create
Burdened for his past he did hate
For the wrong turns and deceits he made
Every other finger was frayed and every other was afraid
He wanted to hold her hands but they were like porcelain and at peace
He did not want to crack them or make them crease
Instead he would just brush pass them
But when he touched them her heart did race
And when he did not she felt misplaced

Writers Blood

I bleed every day in my own secret way
I bleed for all who block out their pain
You must think it is dark and tragic
But I think it is magic
To help and ease everyone's pain
I will take the blame
Pour my heart out onto this page
Leaving it beautifully blood stained

Queen's Quench

Yes I am a Queen on my throne
But sometimes this Queen gets tired of sleeping alone
The person to fill this space can only be a King
I am the yin and has to be my yang
To balance me out and bring harmony
To take away my uncertainties
So until that time comes I am not breaking bread
To just get some crumbs

Less vs More

I am starting to not really care anymore
Is that good or bad? I cannot be sure
I want to care less but I do not want to be careless
I want to not go with my heart but do not want to be heartless
I want to be free but what I have to offer is not cheap
I want to be playful but I am playing for keeps

Unconditional Love

You are more precious to me than any gem, stone or gold
For your health and protection I would sell my soul
I could watch you sleep for days on end dreaming away so peacefully
I could stroke your face and look into your innocent eyes which shine so brightly
I could hold your hand forever to guide you while you grow
Love you forever for you are my heart and soul

The One That Got Away vs The One That Stayed

If there is one that always gets away, what does that mean for the one that stayed?
Are they just a second class grade to the one who could not stay?
Have the true feelings gone away or have they simply just been misplaced?
The trouble with the one that got away is
It leaves you wondering...
Wondering was it all just a masquerade?
Because if it was not then surely they would have stayed

Tremendous Mess

You are a tremendous mess my dear which most would fear
But I could not stay clear
Even though I knew the situation was queer
My heart was calm when you were near
You are a tremendous mess my dear
Even though I should not have I always adhered
But when you left and threw your spear
I became the tremendous mess my dear
Because of you this was very clear

The Heart vs The Ego

You do not want me you never did
You only want me now because I have closed this lid
You created this storm and now you are complaining that it is raining
You are so tiring you are so draining
Your ego may have been bruised but my heart was abused
Love does not break hearts egos do

Amuse Me

Muse needed please apply within:
Must be able to get deep under my skin
Must have the cheekiest grin
Must be my sweetest sin
Must be able to inspire
Must be my deepest desire
Must make me forget about everything and everyone prior
Must be able to make me feel and heal
Only apply if what you can offer is the real deal

Lost

It has been 2 years, 6 months, 11 days and 8 hours since I made my fate
It has been 2 years, 6 months, 11 days and 8 hours when I realised I was late
It has been 2 years, 6 months, 11 days and 8 hours when I made the choice to lose you
It has been 2 years, 6 months, 11 days and 8 hours when I started to abuse
It has been 2 years, 6 months, 11 days and 8 hours I have been hiding the scars
It has been 2 years, 6 months, 11 days and 8 hours since the sky has had no stars
It has been 2 years, 6 months, 11 days and 8 hours I have been a selfish, murdering, heartless bitch for
It has been 2 years, 6 months, 11 days and 8 hours when I made the choice to lose you I also lost apart of myself

Actions vs Reactions

It was 5 years, 7 months and 16 days since he last saw her and sent her away which he regretted each and every day.
He thought to himself "Wow does this woman not age? She looks exactly the same."
It was 5 years, 7 months and 16 days since she last saw him when he sent her away.
She thought to herself "OMG he looks so old, not the bold and confident man I used to know."
He walked over to her cautiously afraid to how she might react
She walked over to him not wanting to react.
She thought to herself "Thank god he let me go, he did me a favour."
He thought to himself "Thank god I have finally seen her."
He did not notice the boy shyly standing behind her until he pulled out his hand to greet her.
He thought to himself "Wow she has so moved on."
She thought to herself "Please leave my son alone...you refused me and threw me out before."
They made general chit chat which made him feel like a prat
They threw little digs here and there
Tit for tat
But all she had to do was smile and he was like a pussy cat.
He wanted to know more
She was looking for the front door,
He wanted to pour his heart out to her but was scared she would still be bitter.
They both made excuses as to why they had to go
It was not like it was a long time ago.
Before he left he bent down to the little boy
But could feel she got annoyed.
He looked back at him and could see something familiar that triggered his brain,
An initialled pendant on a silver chain.
She looked all flustered like when they first kissed
She thought "Shit!" grabbed her son and ran,
He tried to grab her must missed.
He stood dumbfounded and shocked
The girl who was only meant to be a bit fun
Who always spun his heart and his world
From the first day he met her and until now.
He thought to himself "Shit! Was that my son?"

Quotations

"Words will always prove why actions mean so much more."

"Be careful when you push someone away, they might actually like it there and want to stay."

"When you hear something that hurts you, you can hear it a thousand times. But when you see something that hurts you, it can haunt your mind forever."

"It is so hard not to change when so many things and people are changing around you."

"If somebody wants you in their life they will put you there, in the same way if somebody does not."

"Yes it is true no matter how much of a good person you are you will never be good enough for someone who is not ready, but when that person is ready they will not be good enough for you."

"It is all about respect. If you cannot respect me then I cannot love you."

"I may be forward in saying what I want but I will never be backwards in saying what I do not."

"When somebody comes with baggage you help them carry it. Make sure you are not the only one left holding it and become damaged yourself."

"Nowadays it is easier to spot a sinner than a saint."

"I do not need a prince to save me, I want a king to come and claim me."

"A writer's mouth might be closed but their mind is always open and never stops."

"Love does not break hearts, egos do."

"When you are stuck in a situation and you feel like you cannot breathe, sometimes it is best to duck out and leave."

"You have to get rid of the clutter. The stuff that takes up unnecessary space, to make room and replace with greater gifts to embrace."

"You cannot keep chasing what does not want to be caught."

"Two people who are meant to be together will be in the same way as two people who are not, no matter how much you fight it. What is meant to happen will and what is meant to happen will not."

"Under think it…Sometimes do not believe everything you think."

"You should not give to receive but you cannot keep giving yourself to someone who only gives you pieces back. It is not good for your soul and will cause your heart to crack."

"Sometimes the only person that can save you can also be the only person that can kill you."

"Once you have a taste of a real man no other will or can satisfy your hunger."

"Somethings never change unless we do."

"I once fell in love with someone who did not love themselves. The greatest lesson I learnt was to love myself."

"It is better to dream than to sleep."

"Silence means more than any words could ever say."

"Be the kind of person that knows more than they think you do but lets them think you know less."

"Just because someone cannot see your worth it does not mean you are worthless."

"Do not mistake someone's patience for being a pushover. For when your time is up they will not be pulling over for you."

"How can the only person who broke you be the only one that can fix you?"

"Give and forgive but do not fret or forget."

"It is not what you feel for someone that matters anymore, it is how they made you feel that does."

"We all love in different ways, but to feel loved you have to find people who love the way you do otherwise you will not ever feel it."

"Until you start to make the right choices in life your life will never change."

"The only thing consistent in life is its inconsistency."

"You do not need the whole world to love you, only the ones who are your whole world."

"Do not ever let your fears get the better of you, because facing your fears is what makes you a better you."

"Do not hold someone in your arms if your heart is still holding onto someone else."

"Everything is forever changing as are you."

"Saying sorry and asking for forgiveness from someone is not the hardest thing to do…Forgiving yourself is."

"The worst thing you can do to someone who reaches out to you, is leave them hanging."

"The only thing that matters about who used to be is who it made you become."

"Always remember to forgive but never forget to never forget."

"I bend but I do not break, I crease but I do not crumble."

"You have not truly given if you only give to get something back."

"If you have not gone out of your way to hurt anyone intentionally, do not let what anyone says intentionally to hurt you."